**Put Beginning Readers on the Right Track with
ALL ABOARD READING™**

The All Aboard Reading series is especially for beginning readers. Written by noted authors and illustrated in full color, these are books that children really and truly *want* to read—books to excite their imagination, tickle their funny bone, expand their interests, and support their feelings. With four different reading levels, All Aboard Reading lets you choose which books are most appropriate for your children and their growing abilities.

Picture Readers—for Ages 3 to 6
Picture Readers have super-simple texts with many nouns appearing as rebus pictures. At the end of each book are 24 flash cards—on one side is the rebus picture; on the other side is the written-out word.

Level 1—for Preschool through First Grade Children
Level 1 books have very few lines per page, very large type, easy words, lots of repetition, and pictures with visual "cues" to help children figure out the words on the page.

Level 2—for First Grade to Third Grade Children
Level 2 books are printed in slightly smaller type than Level 1 books. The stories are more complex, but there is still lots of repetition in the text and many pictures. The sentences are quite simple and are broken up into short lines to make reading easier.

Level 3—for Second Grade through Third Grade Children
Level 3 books have considerably longer texts, use harder words and more complicated sentences.

All Aboard for happy reading!

For my star of a mom—J.O'C.

To ballerinas everywhere—D.D.R.

Library of Congress Cataloging-in-Publication Data

O'Connor, Jane.
    Nina, Nina, star ballerina / by Jane O'Connor ; illustrated by DyAnne DiSalvo-Ryan.
       p.   cm. — (All aboard reading. Level 1)
    Summary: Nina creates a problem for herself when she tells her friends that she will be a star in the upcoming ballet performance and they misunderstand her.
    [1. Ballet dancing—Fiction. 2. Honesty—Fiction.] I. DiSalvo-Ryan, DyAnne, ill.
II. Title. III. Series. PZ7.0222Ni 1997
[E]—dc20
                                                  96-30741
                                                   CIP
ISBN 0-448-41611-5 (GB) A B C D E F G H I J   AC

ISBN 0-448-41492-9 (pbk) A B C D E F G H I J

ALL
ABOARD
READING™

Level 1
Preschool-Grade 1

Nina, Nina STAR BALLERINA

By Jane O'Connor
Illustrated by DyAnne DiSalvo-Ryan

Grosset & Dunlap • New York

4

Dance class is over.

Nina runs out to Mom.

"Hooray!" Nina shouts.
"There is going
to be a dance show.
Our dance is called
Night Sky."

Mom and Nina drive home.
"Eric is the moon,"
Nina tells Mom.
"The rest of us are stars.
We twinkle around him."

That night
Mom and Nina look
at pictures in the album.

There is Nina the butterfly
and Nina the elf.
"Soon we can put in
new pictures,"
says Mom.
"Pictures of my little star."

The next day at lunch
Nina sits next to Ann.
Nina likes Ann best
of all the girls.
She tells Ann
about the dance show.
"I am a star," Nina says.

"That is so great!"
says Ann.
Then she pokes
Beth and Emily.

"Guess what?" says Ann.

"Nina is in a dance show.

And she is the star!"

"Cool!" says Beth.

"Wow!" says Emily.

"The star!

You must be so good."

Nina does not know

what to say.

She is <u>a</u> star.

She is not <u>the</u> star.

But all the fuss is nice.

So Nina eats her hot dog.

She does not say a thing.

At the next dance class
Nina watches Miss Dawn.

"Point your hands.

Point your feet.

Be pointy like a star,"

Miss Dawn tells the girls.

"Then spin and twinkle

around Eric

the moon."

Nina learns
all the steps.

But sometimes
her feet will not do
what she wants.
And spinning is hard.

"Better,"
says Miss Dawn.

But Miss Dawn
never says "Great"
like she says
to some kids.

Nina is glad
Ann cannot see her.

On Saturday
Ann comes over to play.
They hide out in a cave.

The cave is made of sheets.

It is cold in the cave.

But they must hide
from the bear.

"Grandma called,"
Mom tells Nina.
"She can't come
to the dance show."

Ann looks at Nina.
"Nina, could I come?
I would love
to see you dance."

"NO!" thinks Nina.

"Yes," says Mom.

"Of course you may come."

Now what will Nina do?

That night
Nina cannot sleep.
The show is in three days!
Ann will find out
Nina is not a real star.
Maybe Ann will not like her
anymore.

The next day
Nina has a plan.
It is not a good plan.
But it is the only plan
she can think of.
All day she limps
around the house.

She limps in the supermarket
and at the pizza place.
"My leg hurts,"
Nina keeps saying.
Nina does not look at Mom
when she says this.
She does not like to fib.

That night Nina takes a bath.
"My leg still hurts,"
she says.
"Maybe I can't be
in the dance show!"
Mom looks at Nina.
"Do you <u>want</u> to be in it?"
"Yes!" says Nina.
But then she starts to cry.
Nina tells Mom everything.
Mom tells Nina to tell Ann.
"Ann will understand,"
says Mom.
Nina is not so sure.

At school Nina sees Ann.
"Ann, I have something
to tell you.
I am not <u>the</u> star of the show.
Three other kids are stars too.
It is no big deal."

Ann shrugs.

"So what?

I just want to see you dance."

Then she gives Nina a locket.

It looks like a star.

"I hope you like this.

It shines in the dark."

It is the day
of the dance show.
Mom and Ann are there.

Up goes the curtain.
Nina is a star—
a pretty good star.

And she is the only one
who really shines.